NO-BOT

THE ROBOT'S NEW BOTTOM!

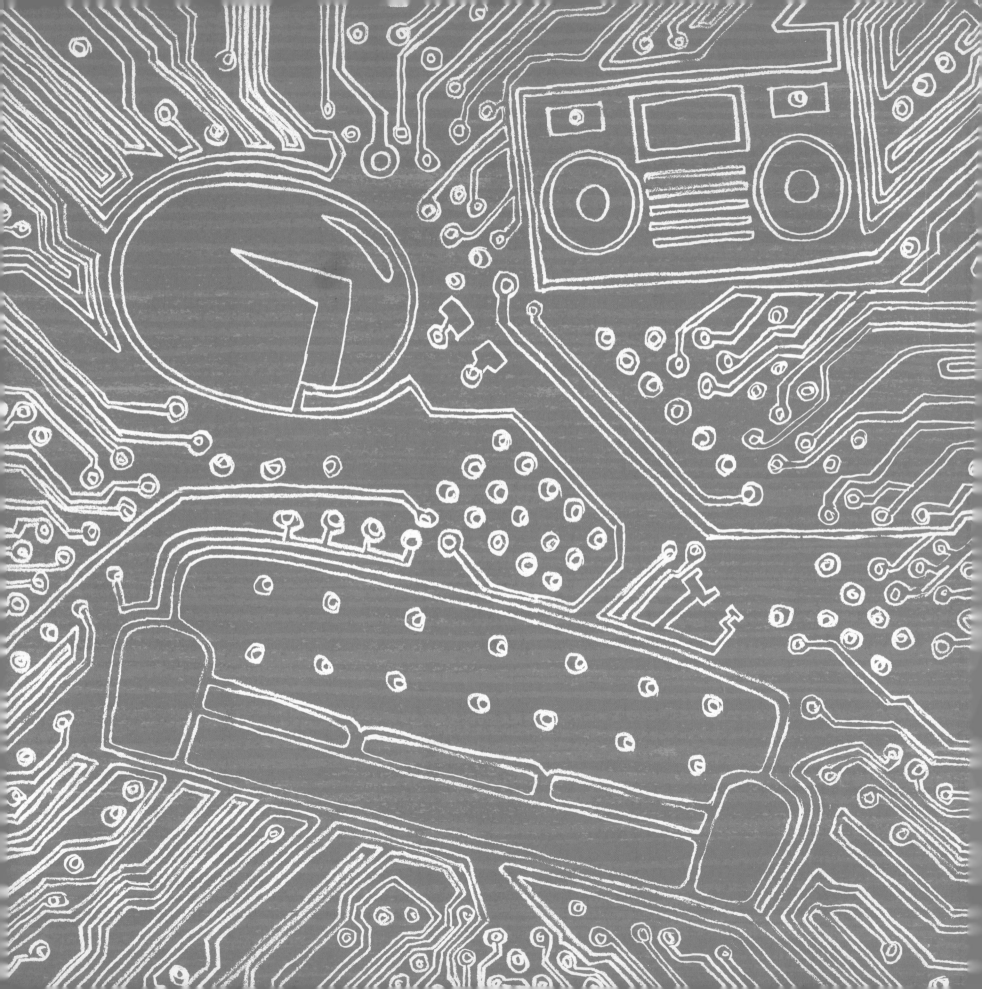

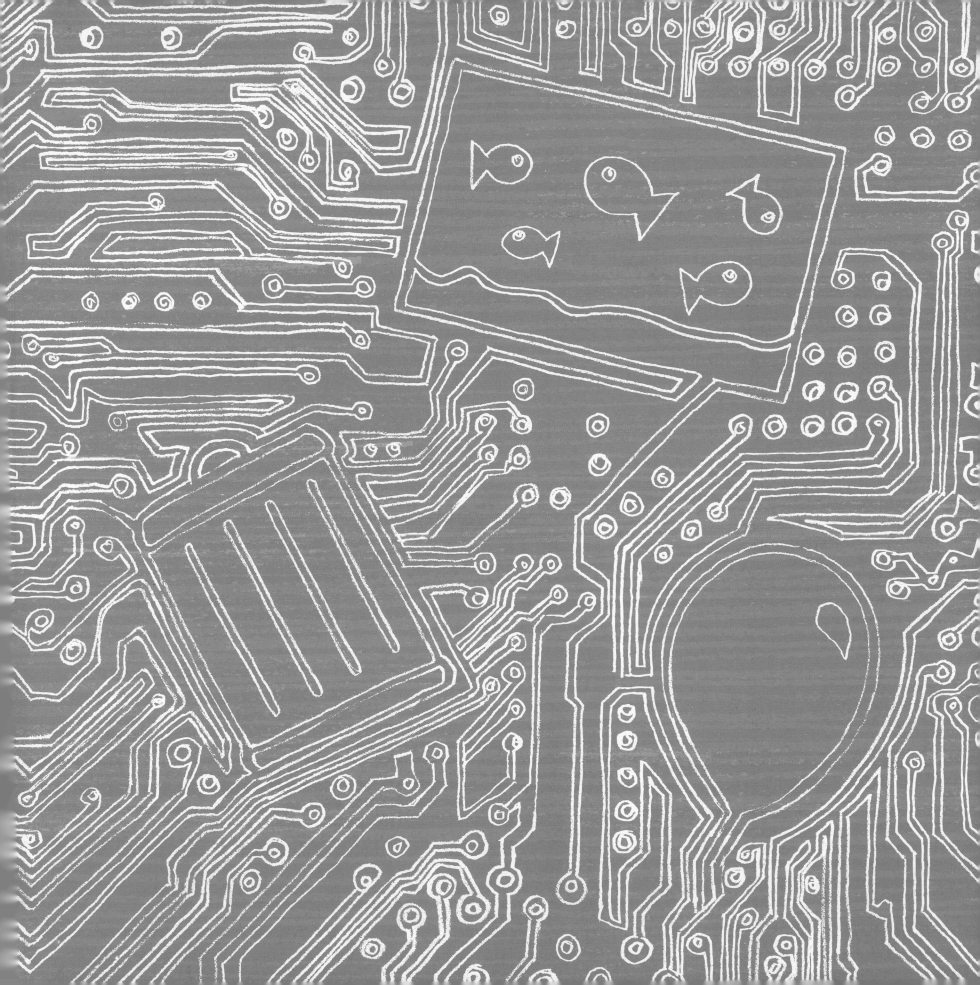

Meet Sue and Paul:

Sue Hendra and **Paul Linnet** have been making books together since 2009 when they came up with *Barry the Fish with Fingers*, and since then they haven't stopped. If you've ever wondered which one does the writing and which does the illustrating, wonder no more . . . they both do both!

To Jane (our brilliant Art Director)
who is calm, kind and sane
when we are being a pain.

SIMON & SCHUSTER

First published in Great Britain in 2020 by Simon & Schuster UK Ltd • 1st Floor, 222 Gray's Inn Road, London, WC1X 8HB

A CBS Company • Text and illustrations copyright © 2020 Sue Hendra and Paul Linnet

The right of Sue Hendra and Paul Linnet to be identified as the authors and illustrators of this work
has been asserted by them in accordance with the Copyright, Designs and Patents Act, 1988

A CIP catalogue record for this book is available from the British Library upon request

978-1-4711-7174-1 (PB) • 978-1-4711-7175-8 (eBook) • Printed in China • 1 2 3 4 5 6 7 8 9 10

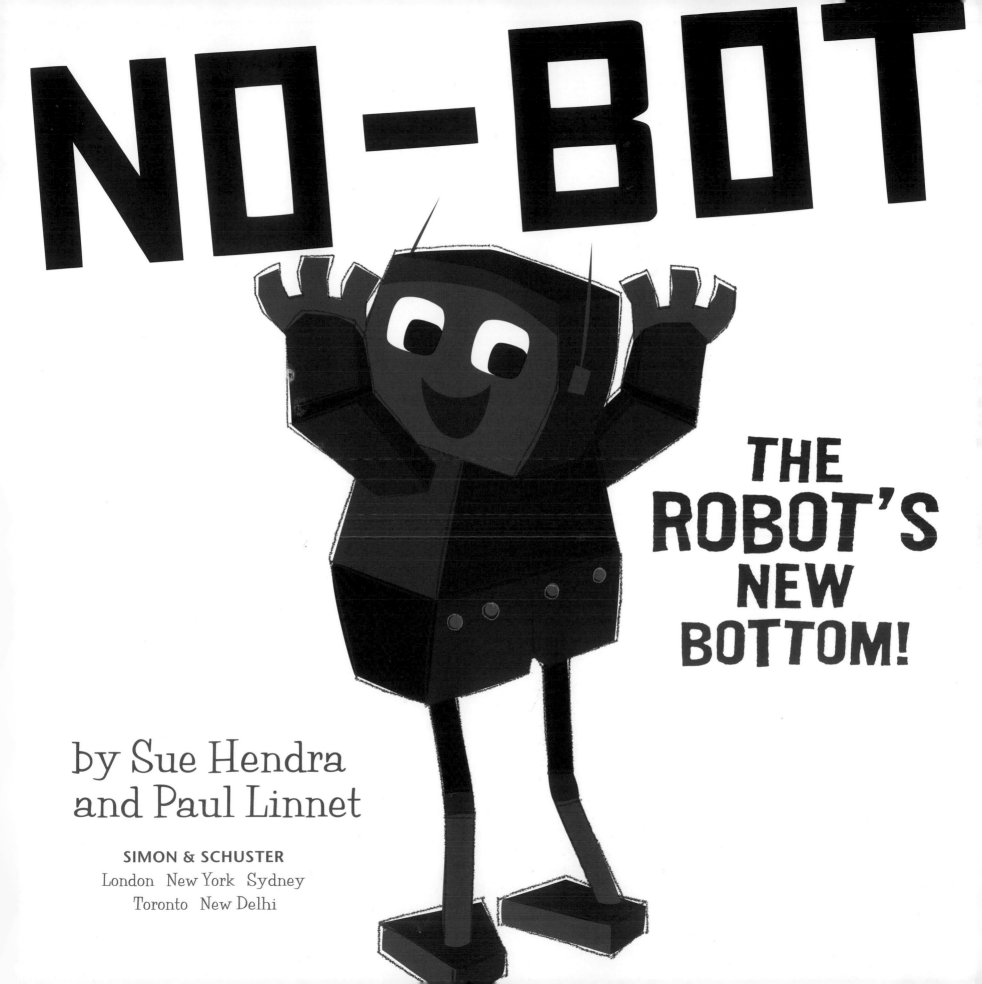

NO-BOT

THE ROBOT'S NEW BOTTOM!

by Sue Hendra
and Paul Linnet

SIMON & SCHUSTER
London New York Sydney
Toronto New Delhi

Bernard the robot loved to go to the park with his friends.

"Come on, everyone, race you to the swings!"

"Wheeeeeee!"
squealed Bernard.

BzZZZzZ.

"Wahooooo!"
he laughed.

CLANK.

"Look at me!"
Thud!
Thud!
THUD!

"Let's all get on
the see-saw."

Squeak, squeak.

"What are all
those funny noises?"
asked Monkey.

"I think they're coming from Bernard's bottom," said Bear.

"MY BOTTOM?"

asked Bernard, surprised.

"Yes," said Bear. "Look – there's smoke and sparks coming out of it!"

"Oh no, you're right!" said Bernard.

"You'd better take it away, Bear, before it explodes!"

So off Bear went with Bernard's bottom.

"How embarrassing," said Bernard.
"I'm supposed to be a robot not a no-bot!"

"Don't worry," said his friends.
"We're going to find you a new bot!"

"Come with me," said Monkey.
"I know what will make a great bottom!"

"Cheese?" said Bernard.
"A bottom made of cheese?"

"Yes!" said Monkey.

"No," said Bernard.

"Mmm, cheese!"

"I like the colour, but NOT the smell."

And it wasn't just Bernard who noticed the smell.

"Can we try something that's comfy to sit on?" asked Bernard.

That gave Bird an idea.

Quite a strange idea . . .

"It's a little heavy," said Bernard.

"Don't worry, Bernard," said Dog. "I've found the perfect bottom for you. It's red and it's lovely and light!"

"HELP!
I'm floating away,"
shouted Bernard.

"Don't worry," said Bird.
"I think I have a way
to get you down!
Just one little peck . . ."

"I can't look,"
whispered Monkey.

The friends kept trying,
but the bottoms they found were either . . .

too noisy . . .

too yucky . . .

or just too weird.

"I've had enough," said Bernard.

"I don't want to try **any more bottoms**."

"Will you try just one more?" pleaded Bear.

"Oh alright," said Bernard, reluctantly.

"I can't believe it!" gasped Bernard.

"It's my old bottom!
You fixed it!
Thank you, Bear."

Bernard was so happy, and so were his friends,
but then they heard something . . .

And everyone chuckled . . .
including Gary!

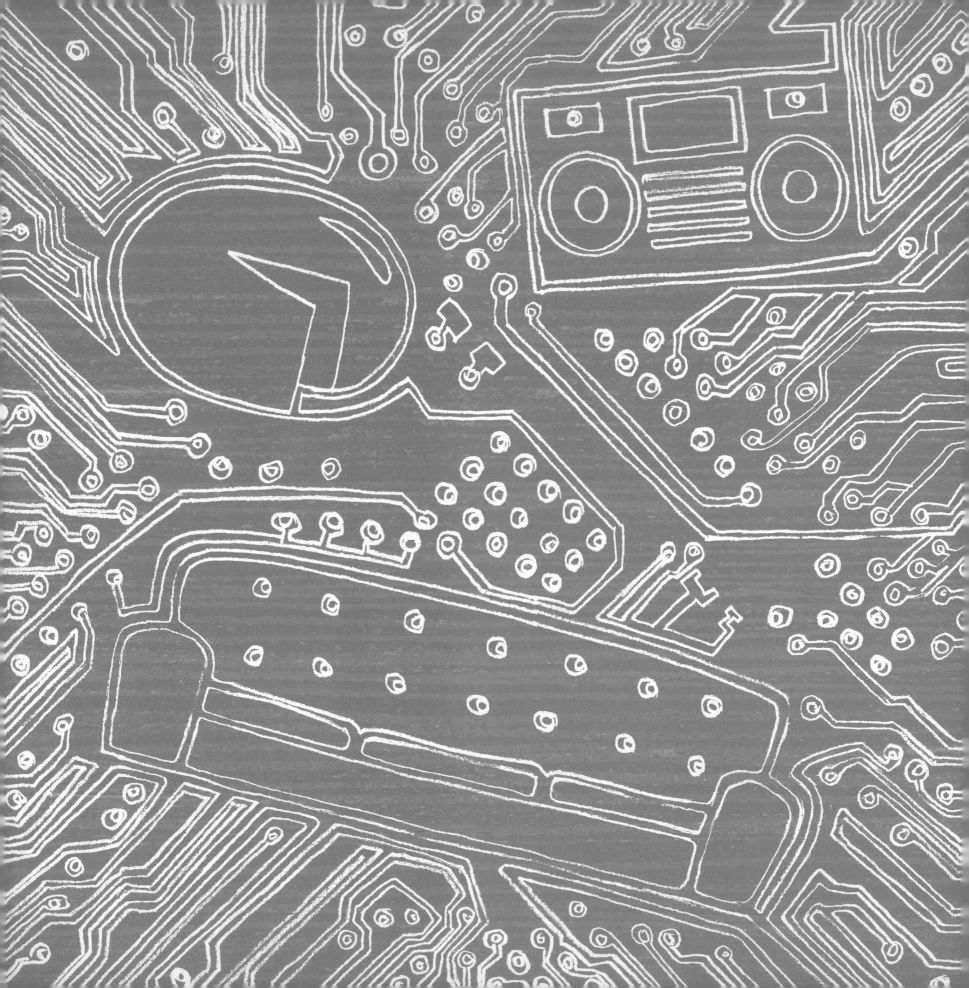

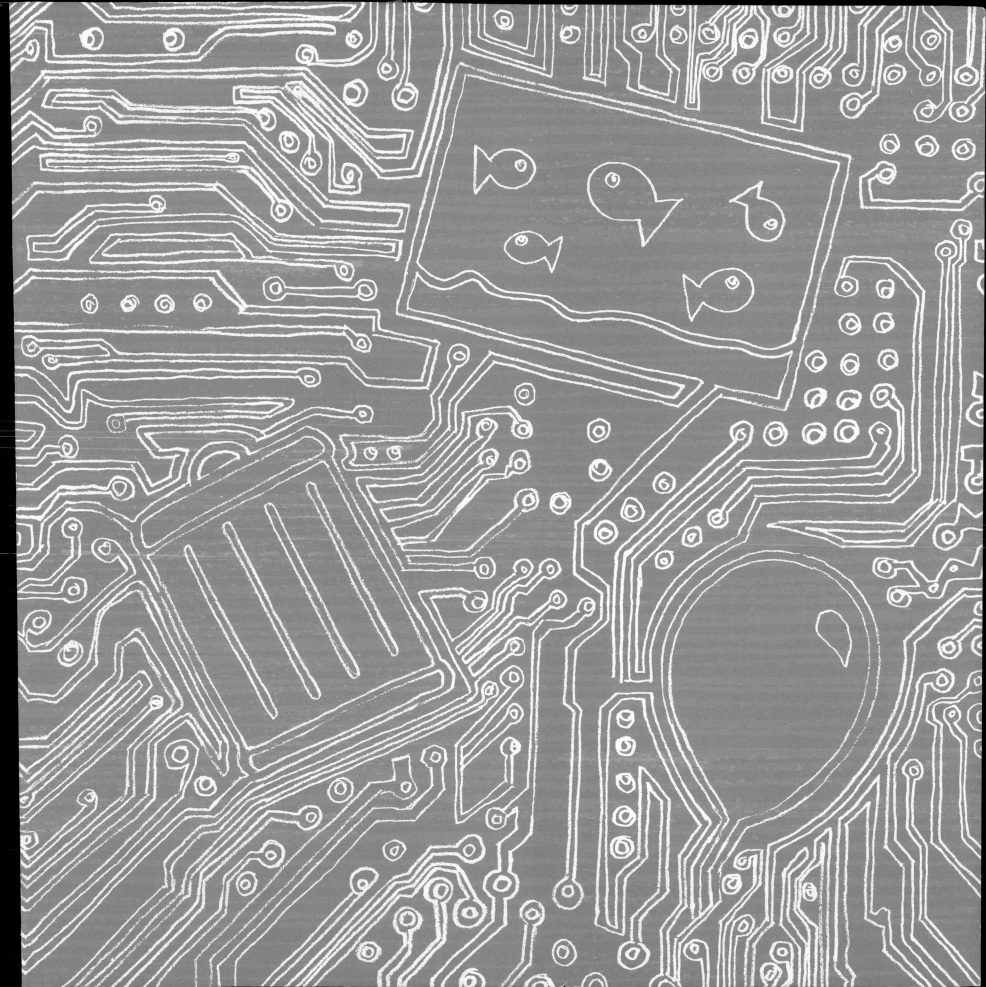

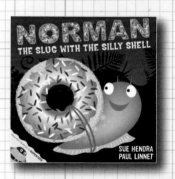

If you like

NO-BOT

THE ROBOT'S NEW BOTTOM!

you'll love these other
adventures from

Sue Hendra and Paul Linnet

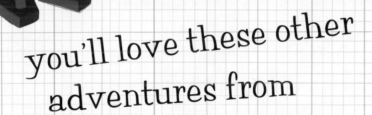